W9-DET-723

BMX

Scott Dick

Heinemann Library
Chicago, Illinois

Designed by Celia Floyd
Originated by Universal
Printed in Hong Kong by Wing King Tong

07 06 05 04 03
10 9 8 7 6 5 4 3 2 1

Library of Congress Cataloging-in-Publication Data

Dick, Scott, 1956-
  BMX / Scott Dick.
      p. cm. -- (Radical sports)
Includes bibliographical references and index.
Summary: An introduction to the sport of BMX, or bicycle motocross, discussing techniques, equipment, safety measures, and competitions.
  ISBN 1-58810-623-3 (HC), 1-4034-0103-9 (Pbk)
  1. Bicycle motocross--Juvenile literature. [1. Bicycle motocross. 2. Bicycle racing.] I. Title. II. Series.
  GV1049.3 .D53 2002
  796.6'2--dc21

J796.6
DIC
7/03

                              2001004800

Acknowledgments

The Publishers would like to thank the following for permission to reproduce photographs: All photos by Neill Phillips except pp. 4, 29b Corbis; and pp. 6, 7, 29a Rich More.

Cover photograph reproduced with permission of Neill Phillips.

Every effort has been made to contact copyright holders of any material reproduced in this book. Any omissions will be rectified in subsequent printings if notice is given to the publisher.

Some words are shown in bold, **like this.** You can find out what they mean by looking in the glossary.

CONTENTS

Introduction 4

What is BMX? 6

The Right BMX Bike for You 8

What Else Do You Need? 10

Checks and Preparation 12

BMX Skills

   Manuals and Wheelies 14

   Bunny Hops and Jumps 16

   Taking a Berm 18

   How to Start a Race 20

Safety and Rules 22

Caring for Your Bike 24

Taking It Further 26

The International Scene 28

Glossary 30

Useful Addresses 31

Further Reading 31

Index 32

INTRODUCTION

A short history

BMX stands for bicycle motocross. The sport of BMX took off in Southern California in the early 1970s, where kids wanted to be like their motocross heroes, jumping and racing their bicycles the way their heroes did on their motorbikes. Since motorcycles were too heavy for most children to handle, the BMX bike was invented.

During the 1970s a range of BMX bikes were developed by companies such as DG and Schwinn, makers of the famous Stingray, and Redline, Mongoose, and GT. The early bikes were heavy and large. The companies soon developed frames made from **chromoly** and aluminum, which made the bikes lighter and stronger.

One of the first BMX races was held in the parking lot of a supermarket in California. Soon after this, the sport became organized. Dirt tracks popped up all over the United States. By the early 1980s BMX racing had spread to Europe and then the rest of the world. The first World Championship of BMX Racing was held in Dayton, Ohio in 1982.

This is an early BMX race from the 1970s.

Riding a BMX is a perfect way to stay healthy and have fun.

Races and competitions

Over the next ten to fifteen years, different styles of BMX riding developed. Racing, where riders ride around a track with jumps and turns, is where BMX riding began as a sport. A more recent variation is BMX freestyle, where riders perfect tricks and skills similar to skateboarding. Freestyle is the general term used for **dirt, street, vert, and flatland** riding. These four types of BMX freestyle allow riders to perform specific tricks and ride in a more unstructured and non-competitive way.

Why ride BMX?

A BMX bike is the perfect sport for anyone who enjoys riding a bike. It provides exercise as well as the joy and freedom of riding. The fun of riding a BMX bike lies in the fact that because they are usually lighter and stronger than other bikes, it is easier to jump, race, and put the bike where you want it to go. BMX riding is a sport that encourages self-expression and fun. Once you are hooked, you will never want to give it up.

WHAT IS BMX?

There are many different types of BMX riding and bikes. You should know about each of them so that you know all that the sport has to offer.

BMX racing

BMX racing takes place on a special track with jumps and banked turns or corners called **berms.** The goal is to get around the track as fast as possible. A race consists of up to eight riders racing a number of laps.

BMX freestyle

Dirt jumping is where riders ride on prepared dirt jumps that are normally bigger than those on tracks. These allow the riders to get big air. Big air is what BMX riders call rising up a long way above the ground.

Street riding is riding alone or with your friends around the streets and trying to pull tricks. Riders use steps, rails, and ledges to **grind**—you grind by moving the **stunt pegs** on your wheels along a metal bar or the edge of a ramp. Street riding can also be practiced at a skatepark or on a specially designed street course that has different types of ramps.

This rider is getting big air on a freestyle dirt jump.

Dave Mirra, a U.S. BMX star, does some vert riding on a halfpipe.

Vert riding, also known as ramp riding, is done on a full skateboard-style halfpipe. A halfpipe is a "U"-shaped wooden ramp with a flat section at the bottom and a platform at either end. Riders get "big air" out of the top of the halfpipe and then are able to pull tricks.

Flatland riding is a competition where riders do all of their stunts and tricks on the ground. Flatland competitions are usually held on pavement.

Getting advice

The best place to start BMX riding is at a local club or track. Most BMX clubs have weekly sessions that you can attend, or specific "starter days" for new riders. They might also organize coaching sessions or rider clinics. Local bike stores should have details on where the nearest BMX track is located. Never be afraid to ask other experienced riders for information when you are at the track. Major bike companies with sponsored riders also run their own rider clinics at tracks and do tours around the country. Your national BMX organization will be able to tell you where the nearest BMX club is located.

Bike size is very important. BMX bikes come with standard 20-inch wheels but the bike frames range in size. A good bike store will advise you on the sizes.

Height	Frame Size
4' and under	mini
4'–4'10"	junior
4'10"–5'8"	pro
5'8"–6'3"	XL
6'3" and up	XXL

TOP TIP

🚲 Getting the right bike is critical. Do not get a bike that is too big for you, or you will not have full control over it. Do not choose your bike based on the color or stickers. Choose your bike wisely.

Make sure you feel comfortable on the bike. You should be able to sit on the seat with your feet touching the floor. You should not have to stretch too far to hold onto the handlebars. If your knees are hitting the handlebars when you ride, the bike is too small.

Handlebars

The handlebars need to be the right width and height to help you control your bike. The bars also need to be in line with the forks—too far back or forward can affect the handling of the bike.

Forks

The forks are made from the same metal as the frame. You will need to have a number plate at the top of the forks for races.

Frame size guidelines

When considering buying a bike you should decide what kind of BMX biking you want to do. There are specific bikes for the different disciplines but some models will allow you to do everything.

A race bike will be lightweight to allow the rider to race around the track faster. It will also have different tires to get a better grip. A **dirt** bike will be heavier than a race bike because it has to be much stronger for jumping, but it can be used for racing. **Freestyle** bikes are also heavier and stronger. They have **stunt pegs** fitted to the axles of the wheels. These allow you to **grind** and give you something to stand on while performing tricks.

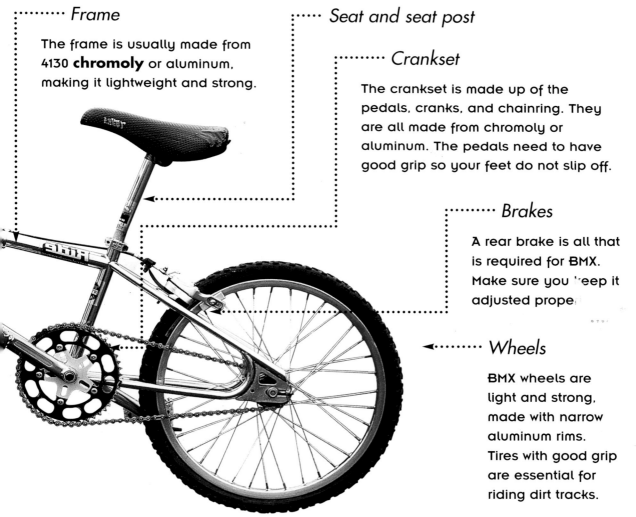

Frame

The frame is usually made from 4130 **chromoly** or aluminum, making it lightweight and strong.

Seat and seat post

Crankset

The crankset is made up of the pedals, cranks, and chainring. They are all made from chromoly or aluminum. The pedals need to have good grip so your feet do not slip off.

Brakes

A rear brake is all that is required for BMX. Make sure you keep it adjusted prope...

Wheels

BMX wheels are light and strong, made with narrow aluminum rims. Tires with good grip are essential for riding dirt tracks.

WHAT ELSE DO YOU NEED?

Basic equipment

Most BMX clubs have helmets and gloves that they rent to riders. Secondhand protective equipment is sometimes sold at races for a great price. Make sure the equipment fits properly, and get advice from an expert before you buy it.

Clothing

For racing, the minimum clothing you will need is a long-sleeve jersey or sweatshirt, and long pants or jeans to protect your arms and legs if you fall. A BMX race shirt is lightweight and vented to keep you cool. It offers protection while riding.

Gloves

A good, strong pair of leather gloves will protect your hands and give you a good grip when riding. They also help prevent blisters.

BMX helmet

A good helmet is important for any form of BMX riding. For **dirt** riding, you need a basic dirt or skateboard helmet. For **freestyle** or racing, you will need a full face helmet for total protection. Your helmet size is critical because helmets can be dangerous if they are too big.

Pad set for your bike

You will also need a pad set for your bike to cover the stem, bars, and the top tube of the frame. These pads will prevent you from hitting yourself (normally your knee) on these parts of the bike while riding.

Elbow and knee pads

This equipment prevents injuries and also makes you feel safer when riding.

Shoes

It is best to wear soft-soled skateboard shoes or tennis shoes to get a good grip on the pedals. More experienced racers are starting to use clip-in pedals with shoes to give them faster acceleration and greater speed.

Checking your bike

You need to make sure your bike is safe and running correctly to achieve the best results. Check to make sure that your chain and wheels are not loose, that you have enough air in your tires, and that your brakes work. Also make sure that your headset and handlebar stem are not loose.

Make sure that you check tire pressure (left) and that your chain is not loose (above).

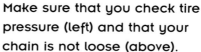

SAFETY FIRST

🚲 Always check your bike before going out to ride. Cover all the basic areas, such as tires, wheels, brakes, cranks, and handlebar stem.

At the track

You can learn a lot from experienced riders. Watch how they take the jumps, **berms,** and lines around the track. Even the best riders watch others if they are having a problem with a certain part of the track. If you can, walk around the track to get a close look at the layout of the jumps and berms. Talk to the other riders to get tips. There are always organized practice sessions at BMX tracks so riders can get acquainted with the track before racing.

Keeping fit and healthy

Before going out to ride, it is a good idea to do some warm-up exercises on your hamstrings, calves, back, and upper body. This will help you warm your muscles and reduce the risk of straining. After a riding session, you can cool down with a gentle ride and some light stretching to prevent stiffness and muscle strain.

Hamstring stretch

Have one leg straight and the other bent. You should feel a stretch along the back of your straight leg. Hold for 10 seconds. Repeat six times for each leg.

Quadricep stretch

Standing on one leg, pull the other up behind you. Hold this position for 10 seconds and then do the other leg.

Upper body stretch

Put your hand under the elbow and push your arm back across the chest and over your shoulder. Then repeat the stretch using your other arm.

Nutrition

Eating the right food before riding or racing is very important. Do not eat a heavy meal right before you go out to ride your bike. Eat something light like cereal, bread, or fruit. While out riding you should eat little but often. Fruit or energy bars are ideal. Be sure to drink plenty of fluids while riding—water is normally best. All these items are light and can be packed in a small bag to take to the track.

MANUALS AND WHEELIES

Now you are ready to ride your BMX bike. Riding a BMX bike is like riding any other bike except you will have more control over the bike. You will also find the BMX bike easier to ride than heavier, larger-wheeled bikes.

Wheelies and manuals

The first tricks you should learn are **wheelies** and **manuals.** These tricks are similar in that they both involve the front wheel leaving the ground while riding.

Popping a wheelie takes some practice. Try the move slowly at first. Practice on a flat surface away from the track. Make sure you are wearing your safety equipment.

1. Lean your body back.

2. Pull up the bike with the handlebars.

3. At the same time, keep pedaling and moving forward.

1. Get your body in the right position and lean back.

2. Lift the front wheel.

Being able to manual is very useful when riding any form of BMX, whether racing or **freestyling.** It allows you to get through jumps on a race track, such as **speed jumps, triples,** or **whoops,** smoothly and quickly without pedaling.

Timing and coordination during this move is crucial. Manuals can take a long time to perfect so be patient and keep practicing.

3. Let the bike glide over the jump while still moving forward.

BUNNY HOPS AND JUMPS

Once you have practiced **manuals** and **wheelies,** you are ready to learn how to do **bunny hops** and clear jumps. There are many different jumps you could face while riding, including **table-tops, speed jumps, triples, whoops** or **doubles,** and a technical section on a BMX track called a **rhythm section.**

Bunny hops

1. Grip your feet on the pedals. To do this, try to curl your feet around the pedals. Practice this standing still, then do it while moving forward.

2. Bend your knees slightly.

3. Lift the bike with both your hands and feet in a bouncing movement.

SAFETY FIRST

Make sure you are wearing all your protective gear while trying these basic riding moves, and at any other time while on the track or the street.

Jumping doubles

This will take some time depending on your ability, strength, and age. Work up to this very slowly and only attempt it when you are fully confident. Try a few practice runs to get the right speed by just riding through the double jump. Too much speed will send you too high and too far, and not enough speed will cause you to hit the second jump. **Pumping** on the downside of the jump will give you more speed to take the next jump or allow you to ride faster along the next section of track.

1. Speed up and use the first jump as your take off point. Lift your bike slightly as you hit the **lip** at the top of the first jump.

2. Aim for the downside of the next jump so that you can land smoothly.

3. Keep your bars straight and your pedals horizontal.

4. Use your knees, arms, and legs to soak up the landing.

TAKING A BERM

A **berm** is a banked and sloped turn on a BMX track. They can be various sizes and angles. Riding a berm correctly can give you an advantage in a race. If you come out of the berm correctly, you will have more speed to take jumps. You may also block another rider from behind or pass a rider ahead of you.

Basic tactics

The path you take on the track is called the line. Practicing the lines you take on a berm is important because following another rider's line will not allow you to pass to get into the lead. There are three basic tactics to riding a berm—high-low for passing, low-high to protect your position, and **railing** (riding as fast as you can) the turn for speed.

High-low

1. Approach the berm high on the outside. This is called riding the **high line.**

2. Gather speed and rail high around the berm until you are near the middle or toward the exit of the berm.

3. Now you are ready to **swoop** down or pass the other rider to the inside.

Low-high

1. Stay low-to-middle of the track on your approach to the berm.

2. Ride up the berm.

3. Ride around, protecting your inside from other riders diving under you.

Railing

Railing as fast as you can, approach the berm through a line from the middle to the top. Gain as much speed as you can on your exit to attempt passing on the next **straight** or to give you better speed and momentum to take a jump.

Try to practice the different berm lines with a few friends at the track. It will be a lot of fun and you will improve your riding skills.

HOW TO START A RACE

The start is the most important part of a BMX race. If you get a bad start, it will be hard to fight your way through the pack. Most top riders practice their starts more than anything else.

The area on a BMX track where you start in a race has a gate that drops down. Most tracks have a light and sound sequence that triggers the gate. The lights are similar to traffic lights with a voice activated command saying "Riders, set 'em up… riders ready… watch the gate or lights."

Getting ready to go

Before you start a race, you will have to line up in your starting position against the gate and wait for it to drop. There are two basic methods of starting a race. For beginners there is the one-footed start, but the more popular method is the two-footed start.

Balance and push up against the gate when waiting for the race to start. Concentrate on the lights and voice commands.

One-footed start

One foot should be on the start pad on the ground by the back wheel. The other foot should be on the pedal. As the gate goes down, the rider throws his or her weight forward while putting the back foot on the pedal and pushing out of the gate.

Two-footed start

For a two-footed start, try to get in a standing position with both feet on the pedals. This is made easier because the shape of the start hill will naturally push your bike into the gate. A good tip is to sit down while arranging your feet on the pedals with your strongest or most comfortable foot forward. Sitting means that it will be easier to balance at first and you will not wobble as much. When you feel stable, stand up, straighten your arms, and move your weight to the back of the bike. Be ready to push out of the gate when it goes down.

To get a snap is to get a good start out of the gate. A holeshot is where the rider holds the lead out of the gate and down to the first jump or to the bottom of the start hill at the beginning of the race.

When the gate drops, throw your body and bike forward and push out and pedal as fast as you can down the start hill.

SAFETY AND RULES

Getting signed up to race

When you get to the track, the first thing you need to do is find out where you can sign up to race. Usually it is inside a small building, a trailer, or maybe even a tent. Here you can sign up and become a member of a club. You will fill in a card with your age, race plate number, category (novice or expert), and date of birth. A club official will always be on hand to help you. You will then be put in a race called a **moto** with other riders of your age and category.

You will start by having three motos. Just after practice, the moto sheets will be posted and you can check to see what race you are in. Make a note of the race number and your three allocated gate positions. An official will call up the riders before their motos. Check the moto sheets after each qualifying round. You need to be on your bike, wearing all of your equipment, at the back of the start hill or pre-staging area at least ten races before your race.

Be safe. Wear all of your safety gear while riding and follow the rules at races.

Safety and rules

BMX is a very exciting and extreme sport, but it can be dangerous if you do not follow some basic safety rules.

Do not ride when you are tired. Most accidents and crashes happen at the end of the day or session.

It is very important to obey the flags at all times.

On race days there will be officials at the track to help with the running of the race. The chief referee on the track will also have two or three marshals to help. They will have three colored flags; red, yellow, and green. A red flag means to stop racing—only the senior referee has this flag. Yellow is to pause a race if a rider is down, and a green flag allows the race to go on.

TOP TIP

- For racing you will have to remove **stunt pegs,** chain guards, reflectors that stick out, and kickstands.

SAFETY FIRST

- Replace any worn or broken equipment on your bike before riding.

- Always wear all the safety equipment every time you ride.

- Always choose a safe place to ride.

- Watch out for other riders at the track or skatepark.

- Always ride the correct way around the race track.

- When racing, always have a full set of pads on your bike.

- Take your time and do not attempt difficult jumps or tricks until you are ready.

- Keep your riding area clean.

CARING FOR YOUR BIKE

Expert riders or other members of a BMX club can teach you how to care for your bike. The most important parts to check are what we call the running gear. This includes the chain, wheels, **hubs,** cranks, chainrings (front), **freewheel (rear sprocket),** and tires.

To help look after your bike, you will need a basic tool kit with 10–15mm wrenches, a set of Allen wrenches, and a pump and puncture kit. You will need the wrenches to tighten wheels and pedals, and Allen wrenches to tighten stems, seat post clamps, etc. Always use the right size tool for your bike or you could damage it.

AF Allen wrench   Tire pressure gauge   metric Allen wrenc

multi-purpose wrench   plastic tire lever   puncture repair kit

Oil your chain regularly, wiping off the excess with a cloth, and check for wear. Your wheels should always spin straight. Check for loose or missing **spokes** and make sure your hubs spin freely. If your wheel rubs against your brake, it is a sign that either your wheel alignment is off or your wheel is buckled. If it is not too bent it can be fixed with a spoke key. Have this done at a bike store by someone who has experience with wheel building.

TOP TIP

Regular cleaning not only makes your bike look good, but is a good way to discover problems with your bike as well. There are special cleaners for bikes, but soap and warm water will do. Never jet wash or hose your bike because water can get into the moving parts and bearings.

The crankset

The cranks should spin freely. Check the nuts on the spindles because cranks have a tendency to come loose. Make sure the front chainring is not bent and that it does not have any teeth missing. Also check the chainring bolts if you have them.

The rear brake

Keep your brakes adjusted and check the pads for wear. Do not let the pads rub on the tire because that will wear them down.

The tires

Check the freewheel for play, slippage, missing teeth, and wear. It is very important that you have the correct tire pressure because this can affect the handling and feel of the bike. Check your tires regularly for wear around the walls and tread. A tire with no tread will puncture easily and will not grip.

TAKING IT FURTHER

National BMX organizations in countries around the world host a junior development program to encourage new young riders into the sport of BMX. Contact them to get more information (see page 31 for details).

There are some guidelines to follow if you want to progress in BMX racing. Just remember that reaching the highest level is not going to happen overnight. As in all sports, you will need to practice and train to become a competent rider. Take one step at a time and enjoy the sport.

This 12-year-old is already an accomplished rider.

Coaching for new riders is available at your local BMX club.

Progressing in BMX racing

1. Find a local BMX club. The club officials and the experienced riders there will give you all the help and information you need to get started. They will help you sign up for coaching, rider clinics, and junior development programs.

2. Go to practice nights and compete in open club races that your club sponsors.

3. Once you become more confident, you can race at regional level and at national series events where you can receive a national or regional ranking at the end of the series. Most countries run regional races where a rider can enter at a novice or intermediate level and work his or her way up to expert when they feel they have the skill and experience. Many clubs use the same structure.

4. Once you get to a level where you have a national ranking your national BMX organization may invite you to race at international events all over the world.

This new rider is practicing his starts and joining in the fun of a BMX race.

TOP TIP

🚲 Riders under the age of 16 need specific advice on training. Get professional advice from a nationally-recognized coach.

THE INTERNATIONAL SCENE

Over the years, BMX has become popular all over the world. Each year the UCI (Union Cycliste Internationale) World Championships are held in various countries around the globe. The UCI is the governing body of international BMX. Most continents, such as Europe, South America, and North America, also hold their own championships.

The sport is huge in the United States, with two national organizations, the ABA and the NBL. Both of these groups run their own national series. The ABA holds the "Grands" every year. This is the biggest BMX race in the world and is attended by thousands of riders.

BMX is also big in Australia. Wade Bootes and Warwick Stevenson are two of the top pros in the world. Stevenson is the 2001 ABA No.1 Pro in the U.S. Australia also has one of the top female BMX racers in the world— Natarsha Williams, was World Champion in Elite Woman in 2000 and is now a champion professional rider in the U.S.

Natarsha Williams of Australia is one of the best female riders in the world.

BMX is popular in Britain and has been an organized sport with a governing body since the early 1980s. There are currently about 40 affiliated BMX clubs in Britain. They host the BCF BMX National Series at various tracks around the country as well as the British BMX Championships. In the 1980s, the Kelloggs BMX series was shown on TV and resulted in getting more people interested in BMX in the UK than at any other time. Great Britain's Dale Holmes is one of the best riders in the world. He was the UCI Elite Men's World Champion in 1996 and 2001 and holds nine World Championship medals.

In addition to BMX races, there are international competitions for **vert, street,** and **dirt** riding. The best ones include the ESPN X Games, the Gravity Games, the Urban Games, and the World Extreme Games. These events have been shown on TV, bringing BMX to a worldwide audience, and making U.S. riders like Dave Mirra and Ryan Nyquist worldwide sports stars.

Great Britain's Dale Holmes was UCI World Champion in 1996 and 2001.

Dave Mirra is one of the most famous and successful freestylers in the world.

GLOSSARY

berm   banked turn or corner on a BMX track

bunny hop   lifting your bike up by gripping the pedals with your feet

chromaly   lightweight tubing made from aircraft metal

dirt   where riders perform jump variations over specially constructed dirt jumps

flatland   where riders perform tricks on the ground

freestyle   all styles of trick riding

freewheel or **rear sprocket**   small cog on the rear wheel that is driven by the chain

grind   to use stunt pegs to slide on the top edge of a ramp or metal rail

high line   riding at the top or outside of the berm

hub   center of the wheel

lip   take off point of a jump

manual   doing a wheelie without pedaling

moto   one of three qualifying BMX races.

pumping   to use a pumping motion to lift and push down on or off a jump to gain more speed; also a term used when riding through a rhythm section, pumping the bike and shifting body weight back and forth to get through it, pulling and pushing the bike up and down

rail   to ride a berm as fast as possible to get maximum speed on the exit

rhythm section   group of jumps placed close together on a track that a rider must pump, manual, or jump through

speed jump   single jump on the track that you ride over

speed wheelie   picking up or lifting the front wheel before a jump

spokes   thin circular metal rods that are attached to the rim and hub of the wheel

straight   section of track that has jumps on it

street   to ride on the street; also a constructed course with various wooden jumps, rails, and quarterpipes representing normal street obstacles

stunt pegs   small pegs attached to the wheel axles to allow grinding and balancing

swoop   to pass another rider on a berm

table-top   jump on a track with a flat top; trick in the air getting the bike horizontal

triples   three speed jumps in a row

vert   halfpipe riding

wheelie   lifting your front wheel while pedaling

whoops or **doubles**   set of two speed jumps on a track that you can ride through or jump

USEFUL ADDRESSES

American Bicycle Association
P.O. Box 718
Chandler, AZ 85244

National Bicycle League
3958 Brown Park Drive, Suite D,
Hilliard, OH 43026

MORE BOOKS TO READ

Deady, Kathleen W. *BMX Bikes.* Minnetonka, Minn.: Capstone Press, Inc., 2001.

Gutman, Bill. *BMX Racing.* Danbury, Conn.: Children's Press, 1995.

Holder, Bill. *BMX Racing.* Dublin, Ohio: Pages Publishing Group, 1995.

INDEX

berms 6, 12, 18–19

bike maintenance 24–25

bikes 4, 5, 8–9, 12

Bootes, Wade 28

brakes 9, 12, 24, 25

bunny hops 16

chain 12, 25

checking the bike 12

chromoly 4, 9

clothes and equipment 10–11

clubs 7, 22, 27, 29

coaching 7, 26, 27

crankset 9, 25

dirt riding 5, 6, 9, 11, 29

doubles 16, 17

elbow and knee pads 11

fitness 13

flag signals 23

flatland 5, 7

forks 8

frame size 8

frames 9

freestyle 5, 6–7, 9, 11, 15, 29

gloves 10

grind 6, 9

halfpipes 7

handlebars 8, 12

healthy diet 13

helmet 11

history of BMX sport 4

Holmes, Dale 29

jumps 6, 15, 16, 17

junior development programs
26, 27

manuals 14, 15

Mirra, Dave 29

motos 22

Nyquist, Ryan 29

pad set 11

racing 4, 5, 6, 9, 10, 11, 15, 18,
20–21, 22, 23, 26, 27, 28

railing 18, 19

rhythm section 16

safety 12, 15, 16, 22, 23

shoes 11

speed jumps 15, 16

starts 20–21

Stevenson, Warwick 28

street riding 5, 6, 29

stunt pegs 6, 9, 23

stunts and tricks 5, 6, 7, 9,
14–15

table-tops 16

tool kit 24

tracks 4, 6, 12, 20, 22

triples 15, 16

tires 9, 12, 25

vert riding (ramp riding) 5, 7,
29

wheelies 14

wheels 9, 24

whoops 15, 16

Williams, Natarsha 28

World Championships 4, 28